THE GIRL IN THE WOODS

A GHOST'S STORY

MICHAEL ROBERTSON

Email: subscribers@michaelrobertson.co.uk

Edited by:

Terri King - http://terri-king.wix.com/editing
And
Pauline Nolet - http://www.paulinenolet.com

Cover Design by The Cover Collection

The Girl in the Woods - A Ghost's Story

Michael Robertson
© 2019 Michael Robertson

The Girl in the Woods - A Ghost's Story is a work of fiction. The characters, incidents, situations, and all dialogue are entirely a product of the author's imagination, or are used fictitiously and are not in any way representative of real people, places or things.

Any resemblance to persons living or dead is entirely coincidental.

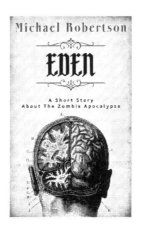

PROLOGUE

B art had offered to drive, but Liz preferred him in the passenger seat, focusing. Doing his job. She'd given him control of her car once. Never again. Maybe they were already there and she hadn't noticed, but the morning after, she'd discovered several more grey hairs.

Useless as a driver, Bart was a great help otherwise. The kid showed initiative and, most importantly, he had the gift. If he worked hard on his personal development, he'd become a truly great medium.

For a lot of the journey, Bart closed his eyes and leaned back in his seat. When he straightened up, Liz eased off the gas. The way of his gift, Bart thrust an arm across her, pointing at a secluded driveway on the right. "In there."

"*There?* Are you sure?" The track looked like a bridleway.

"Stop testing me, Liz. You already know where we're going. I got it right, didn't I?"

"This is certainly the right area, but are you sure that's the best route?"

"Yep. They said it was an abandoned building, didn't they?"

Bathed in shadows, the small road would even have

appeared hostile in broad daylight. Liz shook her head. She flinched when Bart laid his hand against the top of her left arm. "It's okay to be scared of the dark, you know."

"But I'm a medium!"

"A medium who's been briefed about what we're heading in to. There's things much scarier than ghosts out there."

Liz sighed, indicated, and then guided the car into the narrow turn.

The tyres crunched and popped as they trundled over what had once been an asphalt driveway. Years of neglect had turned it in to a crumbling mess of small black rocks. The large pool of white from the car's headlights showed the tufts of grass stubble pushing through the cracks. Long branches leaned over them, the canopy forming a natural tunnel and turning the already dark night darker.

The muscles in Liz's right leg tensed, but she fought the urge to accelerate and kept the car moving at around ten miles per hour. No plans on slowing down, but any faster and she might do permanent damage to her vehicle. An inky blackness on either side because of the thick woodland, she stared straight ahead. "It's been a long time since this driveway saw regular use."

"They might be less than useless most of the time," Bart said, leaning forwards as if it would help him see better, "but at least the police have been down here before us."

"*If* you've guided us to the right place, and *if* they came in this way."

A few seconds later they emerged from the dark woodland tunnel. Liz gasped and pulled her foot off the gas, slowing them to a crawl.

"Are you okay?" Bart said.

"And I thought the driveway was bad. How did we not see this building from the road?" An old institution made from crumbling red brick, it looked like it might have once been a school, a hospital, or …

"It used to be an asylum," Bart said. The glow of a screen lit up next to her, and Bart read from it. "It's been abandoned for —" he paused, his mouth playing out the mental arithmetic "— thirty-eight years."

"Longer than I've been alive," Liz said.

"Is it?"

"I'm not *that* old."

"I'm sorry, when people get over thirty, I can't tell anymore."

Liz stabbed the brake, sending Bart lurching forwards. "Next time you say something like that, I'll bury your teeth in the dashboard." Back to a slow crawl, she leaned forward to look up at the tall building, the moon running a silver highlight across the crumbling ruins.

Four police cars sat in front of the grim institution. They were all turned sideways, their spotlights angled at the building. While illuminating some parts of it, the shadows by comparison turned tangibly dark.

"I hope the others leave us alone tonight," Liz said. "I could do without having to counsel centuries' worth of tormented souls. The one we're about to meet will be bad enough. What was his name?"

"Andy Stick."

"Sounds like a character from a nineteen forties comic strip."

Bart laughed.

The squeaky brakes wound Liz's shoulders tight as she stopped the car. She and Bart got out and approached the nearest police officer.

A short and squat man in his mid to late forties, he had the appearance of someone who still considered himself a young buck despite his double chin, crow's feet, and flecks of grey at his temples. Standing with a board-straight back and raised chest as if the world watched him, his top lip raised, hanging somewhere between a snarl and a sneer, he looked Liz up and down. A misogynist and a sceptic: the worst kind of combination. "I didn't call you in, you know?"

"I know, calling me in is well above your pay grade. I'd imagine someone like you would have to put in a written request just to get a new pencil. Do you still put your hand up when you wanna pee-pee?"

The officer's face flushed red and Bart giggled. "You got a problem, boy?"

Liz stepped between Bart and the officer. For what good it did. With Bart being six feet and four inches tall and her only five feet two, the officer didn't have to break eye contact with him.

At least a minute passed before the officer finally put a leash on his ego and fixed on Liz. "What are you, some kind of ghost whisperer?"

Liz drew a deep breath, dragging in the reek of autumn. Dead leaves, wet mud, rotten wood, and something else. The metallic tang of blood? Or maybe just the memories of it. Hard to tell which timeline her senses were tuning in to. Now she'd made him wait, she returned her attention to the policeman. "You seem to have a lot of questions, Officer ..." She looked down at the badge on his breast and smirked.

If he'd been red before, Officer Cock turned several shades deeper. "Yeah, whatever. Laugh it up, why don't you?"

Bart peered over Liz and laughed too.

Liz didn't think he could stand any straighter until he did. An even more erect Officer Cock drew in a sharp sniff. "How old are you both? Twelve?"

"Look," Liz said. "As much as I want to help you work out

whatever issues you have going on"—she looked down at her wrist despite there being no watch there—"how much longer will this take? We're being paid by the hour, and I'm sure your boss would love to be invoiced for a hefty amount because *Cock* wouldn't let me in."

"Because you'd been Cock blocked," Bart said and they both giggled.

Where he looked like he might have said more, Cock tightened his jaw as if clamping onto his response. A second later, he stepped aside.

Despite the heat of open hostility burning into her as she passed, Liz didn't give Cock the satisfaction of looking back.

NEARLY EVERY WINDOW ALONG THE FRONT OF THE OLD institution had either been smashed or was covered in an impenetrably thick layer of dirt. Vines clung to the walls as if they kept the building upright. The gaping entrance must have once been barred by a large door, but not even the hinges remained. It left a yawning mouth, inviting them to enter the gullet of the beast. Liz bit down against the chill running through her, the night colder than it had been a few seconds previously. Small clouds of condensation spread from her nostrils.

Bart turned on a torch and handed it over before he flicked on another one for himself.

The crack and pop of breaking glass beneath her steps, Liz entered the building, trying to see more than her torch would allow as she ruffled her nose against the damp smell of rot. "Watch where you step. It sounds like there's a basement beneath us, and these floorboards don't smell too stable."

Like with most abandoned buildings, the old asylum

seemed to be holding its breath as if in preparation to show Liz everything it had to offer. The hairs lifted on the back of her neck and she blinked against the darkness. Spirits could be shy, but when they came, they often came in waves.

A few metres along the first corridor—their steps still issuing the same hollow thud from the space beneath them— Bart pointed his torch into a room on their left. Darker than many of the other rooms and filled with the rusty remains of bed frames—the skeletons of a long-abandoned ward—he said, "He's in there."

A shake of her head, Liz snorted a laugh. "I suppose he would be, eh?" After a deep breath, the dust motes in the air dancing in the torch's beam and turning her throat dry, she said, "There's no point in putting it off. Come on then."

There were many windows in the room, all of them covered in sheets save one. A bar of moonlight shone through the dirty glass. It revealed the corpse and the extent of his fatal injuries. Liz's stomach turned. "I've never seen someone who's been cannibalised before." Her mouth dried and the slightest tug of her gag reflex lifted in her throat. A large hole in his stomach, the edges of it had small arches made by human teeth. "He's covered in other people's DNA, but they can't find a match on their system for any of it."

If Liz looked at him for much longer, she'd vomit. It always helped to understand how the victim had died, but she'd not come here for that. The spirit of the man stood beside his inanimate physical form, staring down at what he'd once been.

"Um," Liz said and the man looked up at her, his eyes widening. "Andy, is it?"

Andy fixed on her. It had taken some time for her to get used to them never blinking. But why would they? Dead eyes never dried.

"I'm Liz, and this is Bart." The boy waved. "We're paranormal investigators and we've come to speak to you. Firstly, I'm sure you've worked it out by now, but you're dead."

Although Andy's eyes couldn't glaze, a deep sadness swelled within them as if they had. He frowned.

"I'm sorry," Liz said. "But we want to help you."

Andy scowled.

Liz pressed her palms together, imploring him. "Please let me explain."

But Andy wasn't listening to her anymore. Staring through her, his mouth fell open, he shook his head, and his legs buckled at the knees, throwing him to the floor.

"Andy, please," Liz said and stepped forwards.

"Um, Liz," Bart said.

"Not now."

"I don't think being dead is what's upset him."

"What are you talking about?"

When Bart pointed behind her, Liz turned. The curious spirit of a small girl stood just metres away. She couldn't have been any older than ten. Words abandoned Liz as she looked into the girl's cold and listless eyes. The girl stared straight back.

Twenty-Four Hours Earlier

ANDY USED TO HAVE A RULE THAT HE DIDN'T DRINK COFFEE after midday. Disciplines that were once important seemed so trivial now. The smallest splash of milk turned the black liquid dark brown. The action of stirring it sent him into one of his many daydreams. So dark outside, the bright glare of the kitchen lights turned the window in front of him into a mirror. A fatter and more jaded man than he'd been three years previously stared back. The eyes he recognised; he connected with their sorrow every waking moment. The wrinkled and slightly chubby face that housed them could have belonged to anyone. It would have been easy to draw the blinds, to rid himself of the repulsive reminder of what he'd become. Instead, he sighed, sat at the breakfast bar, and toasted himself by lifting the steaming mug to his lips.

Since they'd renovated the kitchen, Andy spent most of his time in there. Like many of their friends, they were in their forties and deep into a mortgage they somehow paid as if in defiance of mathematical possibility. The extra work they'd done inside the house had given them debts that would probably outlive both of them, but at least they had black marble worktops, an Aga, and white tiled flooring. When they bothered to tidy, it looked like it belonged in the glossy brochures that had convinced them of the need to spend thirty grand in the first place.

Andy's back tightened and his shoulders lifted to his neck at the sound of Chesky's approaching footsteps. Not that she'd bring any expectation with her. She'd come in, get what she wanted, and leave again. No eye contact and no conversation. At least, that was how it normally played out. But there was a difference today. The heels of her flat shoes reported a purposeful click. When she entered the room, she opened and slammed shut several cupboards. When she'd gone through what felt like the entire kitchen, she hovered nearby.

The hard press of Chesky's stare boring into the back of his head, Andy glanced at her in the window's reflection as if his wife had become the Gorgon he now imagined her to be. Her wavy blonde hair an approximation of Medusa's snakes. But she couldn't turn this already granite man to stone. "Just say it. Whatever it is."

The reflection in the window stepped back. She'd clearly come into the room intending to initiate the conversation. After all, experience had given her that expectation. It took a good twenty seconds before she finally spoke. "My patience has run out, Andy."

It didn't come as a surprise, yet her words still tied a knot in Andy's guts and his breathing caught in his throat. Maybe the worst way to calm his stomach, he took a sip of his bitter and scalding coffee. It stung his mouth, and when he swallowed, the muscles in his neck tightened from the strong bitter taste.

His attention back on his mug, it took for the screech of the stool opposite him for Andy to look at his wife. No more than two feet of black marble separated them. They hadn't been this close in a long time other than in passing. At first they'd opted for separate beds in the same room. Then separate rooms. Now they couldn't even bear to look at one another. Had they been able to afford it, they would have probably gone as far as living in separate houses, pretending nothing was wrong while they did their best to ignore the other's existence. Instead, they spent everything they had and more on a new fucking kitchen. Like that would fix everything. And whether it had taken three years or thirty, the inevitable moment had finally arrived.

Chesky shrugged. "I've tried as hard as I can. I've done everything our marriage counsellor suggested."

Where his image had stared back at him from the window, Andy now looked at his wife. A face he no longer loved housed eyes that could have been his own. The reminder that she hurt just as much. He dropped his attention to his coffee.

"I think I'm finally admitting defeat?"

Definitely a question. Should she admit defeat?

"It's ruined us, Andy. I promised myself I'd give it a few years. I mean, we were bound to be fucked up from it. Who wouldn't be?"

Another sip of the strong coffee.

"But I've given three years of my life waiting for you to open up. I've dealt with what happened on my own. I figured you needed to do the same. I've given you space, but you're no further along than when it happened."

There were words in his head. A whole host of words so loaded with poison and toxicity they'd corroded his insides. If Andy let the dam break now, he'd lose his sanity with the outpouring. The nonsensical babble would push everything in his life away from him. Further away than they already were.

She was right; he'd held on to it all for the past three years. He hadn't known where to start then, so how could he possibly know where to start now? Another deep gulp of his scalding drink.

"No matter what I try or say, *nothing* is moving us forward. We've stagnated for the longest time. Actually, *you've* stagnated for the longest time. I can't wait around anymore. I've given you everything I can, and now I need to look after myself."

The weight of what had happened three years ago pushed down so hard on Andy he now had a permanent stoop. Old before his time, he'd need a cane before he turned fifty.

"I'm not saying you should forget. We'll never forget. I'm not saying it shouldn't hurt." Her voice cracked when she said, "Fuck me, does it hurt. But we need to keep functioning as human beings; otherwise, what's the point?"

Andy stared at his soft, pale hands. A lifetime of office work and increasingly less exercise had rounded his edges.

"Are you even listening to me?"

A flash of something rose inside him and he glared at his wife of fifteen years. His fingers twitched with the need to ball his fists. He saw Chesky glance down at them. Something about the way her eyes widened told him she wanted him to react. To show her something other than this withdrawn husk of a human being he'd become. But Andy shrugged and let his hands loosen. "Of course I'm listening to you. I'm not deaf."

After a heavy sigh, Chesky said, "I have no doubt you're hearing me, but it doesn't feel like you're listening. Do you know what it's like to be ignored for three years? To be treated like I don't fucking exist? There's a hole in my life and I've given up waiting for it to be filled."

The heat from Andy's mug burned his grip as he clung on to

it. He spoke through gritted teeth. "You think there isn't one in mine too?"

"A hole where *you* used to be, Andy. We need to find a way to move forward."

Words sat in a jumbled and chaotic mess in Andy's mind. He sifted through them, looking for something. A nugget of coherence. A shred of truth. When he found it, the glare of it dazzled him, but he gave it to Chesky anyway, unpolished and unfiltered. "I'm not sure I can move forward."

Where there had been the sharp penetration of rage and accusation, Chesky's blue eyes now softened and filled with tears. Her mouth bent out of shape and it took her a few seconds to reply. "Thank you."

"Wh-what for?"

"For being honest. No matter how much I don't want to hear it, it's the truth. At last. I worried you wouldn't be able to move on, but I needed to be certain. I needed to know I'd done all I could. Thank you for releasing me."

The ice in Andy's heart melted as he looked at the woman he once loved. He drew a deep sigh into his tight chest. He found three more words in the mess that had rendered him emotionally mute. "So that's it?"

Chesky nodded, tears now running freely down her face. "That's it. We did what we could, eh?"

As Andy's marriage got to her feet and walked from the room, he did the same thing he'd done for the past three years: he sat there and watched it happen.

THE CAFFEINE IN ANDY'S SYSTEM TURNED HIS GRIP ON THE steering wheel clammy, and his pulse beat double time. His stomach a clenched fist, he blinked repeatedly, but it did little to relieve his itching eyes. The car's main beam lost its battle against the almost impenetrable darkness closing in from the woodland on either side of the narrow country lane.

After Chesky made her feelings clear, he hadn't spoken. What did she want from him? That he should beg her to change her mind? Although maybe what she'd given him was the chance to open up. One last opportunity before she slammed the door on their relationship for good. Maybe he should have told her he loved her and that he'd fight for her. That he'd change and express himself better. Maybe he should have been more attentive and loving over the past three years, and maybe he should have promised he would be from that moment forward. He'd be the man she'd fallen in love with. But, truth be told, that man had gone. It wouldn't be fair to ask her to wait for someone who'd never return.

During the day, the woodland on either side of the road would often show Andy red kite, deer, rabbits … Years ago, he'd drive so slow it would send Chesky nuts, but he loved the country, and if he couldn't take in every second of it, then why were they living there? She rarely saw it that way, placing punctuality over pleasure. But at night it turned into something else entirely. The invite for him to explore got rescinded after dark.

Andy returned his attention to the road ahead. The black asphalt lit by his wide main beam, he squinted to ease his tired eyes. For what good it did. They'd stung for the past three years with tears he still couldn't cry. Or maybe refused to cry. If he started, he'd never stop.

The three-note melody of Andy's ringtone blared through the speakers, a pang in his chest from where his already quickened pulse accelerated. The screen in his car's central console mirrored the display on his phone. It read *Home*.

Although Andy reached out, he stopped an inch short of pressing the green button. The plinky plonk of his cheery ringtone continued in stereo, a chirpy announcement to what would be another gut-wrenching conversation. Another reminder of his failings. His inability to maintain a relationship with even himself let alone anyone else.

A deep sigh, Andy pressed the button, if for no other reason than to silence the sound. Because he'd been staring at the bright screen, when he looked up, the glare remained in his vision. He eased off the gas to give him time to regain his night vision.

Chesky finally spoke, talking over the quiet hiss that showed their call to be connected. "Andy?"

"Yep."

"It's going to be like that, is it?"

"You said that's how it's been for the past three years, so why change now?"

A heavy sigh and Chesky said, "Don't blame me for your behaviour. All I did was call it out."

Andy's knuckles ached from his grip on the wheel. The vibration of the tyres against the road ran through his hands and up his forearms.

Chesky spoke with a softer tone. "Please understand, I've tried everything. I didn't want it to come to this, but I'm not sure where else we can go."

"You've made your choice."

"*You* made a choice *every day* for the past *three years!*"

"So that's what this is?"

"What are you talking about?"

"You've called to make yourself feel better about being a heartless bitch. You want to put all the blame on me and expect me to let you? That way, you can walk away from this with a clear conscience. You can now go and hop into bed with whomever you please. You gave me my chance; now you can finally move on."

"This isn't about me having *sex* with someone else. This is about me not having the energy to be in a relationship with *you* anymore. *You* were the one who gave up. *You* lay down a long time ago. I've had to make this decision for the sake of my own sanity."

"You didn't *have* to." The echo of his words rang through Andy's mind. God, he sounded pathetic. So desperate to hold on to a broken relationship. Maybe she'd done him a favour. He'd be miserable whether with her or not.

"Do you know, you've just said more to me on this phone call than you have in the past month?"

Andy pressed his lips tight and breathed through his nose.

"Anyway, what I wanted to say is I hope you find everything you deserve. You're a good man with an open heart—when you let yourself open it. You have a lot to give, so don't deprive yourself by not giving it. Don't spend the rest of your life alone because you can't face what's happened."

"How can I *ever* be happy?"

"I'm not sure I'm the right person to answer that. But if I ever think of anything that'll help, I'll be sure to let you know. Goodbye, Andy."

The click of the call disconnected through the car, and Andy's entire frame sank, deflating with his long sigh.

AT SOME POINT ANDY WOULD FIND A HOTEL. AT SOME POINT, when the tears stopped, when he could see straight, and when he had it in him to talk to a receptionist. One room for one night. Five simple words, but they were beyond his reach for now. And it wouldn't be one night. One night every night for the rest of his life. A hotel. A bedsit where he had to sleep beside an oven. An old people's home. Whichever form it took, his destiny stretched ahead of him, a cheap, lonely, and uncomfortable accommodation providing the perfect metaphor for his existence.

But for now, Andy would drive. He glanced down at the speedometer; the digital blue dial blurred through tears he should have cried three years ago.

Forty miles per hour.

The trees flashed past on either side. The dense press closed in as if the faster he went, the tighter the road became. Impenetrable darkness sat just beyond his headlights' glow.

Forty-five miles per hour.

He'd find a room in a cheap hotel eventually. Somewhere utterly lacking in soul and personality. The genesis of his new beginning.

Fifty miles per hour.

Shit television until three in the morning. Shit television with the volume turned up so loud the neighbouring rooms would complain. But he didn't care because he needed something to drown out his internal narrative. Self-loathing screamed through him with the velocity of a guitar solo at a rock concert. Maybe he'd pay for porn. He'd definitely pay for porn, his laptop back at the house with the life he'd abandoned. He could wank his way towards feeling something. It might help him sleep. If not, he'd drink the minibar dry.

Fifty-five miles per hour.

If he'd have said no, she would have listened. As final as her words were, he knew Chesky. She'd laid down the last chance and given him the option to fight one last time for everything they'd built together. But as much as he'd wanted to, he couldn't. The words were lost in the jumbled mess of his mind. Or maybe they weren't. Maybe he wanted her to leave. If no one loved him, then he didn't have to love himself. If he didn't love himself, he didn't have to heal himself. And therein lay the problem. He knew that. He'd known it for years. Deep inside him sat a box. A box he'd locked three years ago. If he peered inside, he wouldn't ever be able to close the lid again. If he wanted to reconnect with his wife, he'd have to peer inside.

Sixty miles per hour.

The trees were a blur.

The long dark road wouldn't stay straight forever.

Sixty-five miles per hour.

Grief sat as a tumour in his throat. A rock that would swell to the point of choking him. Swallowing sent stabbing pains into his chest. Maybe deer would run out. Maybe he'd become an urban legend, a tale of caution to those who drove too fast.

One ran across the road and he didn't slow down. He hit the second—the larger and slower of the two. Its legs went straight through the windscreen and it panicked. It kicked and kicked. Its hard hooves turned his face to mush as they beat through the front of his skull.

Seventy miles per hour.

They say he was on his way to collect his lottery winnings. So excited, he drove too fast. He had no loved ones. The prize remains unclaimed. They searched the wreck but couldn't find the winning ticket. To this day, no one has found it. But if you're on that road at midnight, it's rumoured that you can hear the shriek of car tyres.

The far reach of the car's full beam showed the bend in the road.

Seventy-five miles per hour.

Andy wrung the steering wheel and pressed harder against the already floored accelerator, the muscles in his right thigh aching from the pressure.

Eighty miles per hour.

They say a tree's the worst thing to hit in a crash. Trees don't yield, whereas cars, especially modern cars, are designed to fall apart. There's only ever one winner. A tree's the best thing to hit in a crash.

Eighty-five miles per hour.

He might be letting his tears out after all this time, but the words wouldn't ever come. How could he possibly begin to articulate his feelings? Language fell woefully short as a form of expression. Andy reached down, his seatbelt unlatching with a quiet but definitive *click*.

Ninety miles per hour, the trees hurtling past him at a nauseating speed.

Anything had to be better than the shame. Of telling friends … well, he didn't have any friends left, but he could already see his mother's face when he tells her his relationship's fallen apart like everything else in his pathetic life. And she'd blame Chesky. And he'd let her. Simply because it would be easier to. The path of least resistance. It wasn't like his mum would ever see her again. So maybe, just this once, he should take charge of his own destiny. For the first time in years he could play an active role in his fate.

Ninety-five miles per hour. The tyres hummed and the steering wheel wobbled. Pains streaked up either side of his face, his jaw clamped so tightly his gums ached.

Besides, he didn't have it in him to go through the courts, arguing over every possession like filling a storage unit with bad memories would somehow restore his self-respect.

Ninety-eight miles per hour. He watched the speedometer, barely able to see the numbers through his tears.

This way had to be better. A deep breath to fill his lungs, his nose clogged with snot.

Ninety-nine miles per hour.

A flash of white on the left—hard to tell what at this speed —but instinct took over and Andy stamped on the brake. The car's ABS sent a machine-gun stutter through his body, the wheels locking for the final few metres.

Now he'd stopped, Andy sat in the driver's seat panting while staring at the trees he'd come so close to colliding with. The wall of immovable trunks formed a militant line, standing before him in judgement. When he looked in his mirror, the wall of black revealed nothing of what he'd seen. He threw the car into reverse and accelerated backwards.

The breath left Andy when he pulled level with the flash of light. Although, not a flash of light. A flash of white. A white nightie. A white nightie on a girl no older than about ten years old.

As Andy sat in his car, the heat from the blowers stinging his already sore eyes, he focused on the little girl in the dark woods. She stumbled and tripped through the undergrowth, walking as if drunk. He worked his jaw, limbering up to say something before he finally managed, "What the fuck?"

THE GIRL'S WOBBLY PATH THROUGH THE WOODS APPEARED completely lacking in intention as she veered one way and then the other. Such a pure sight in such a dark setting, it turned a cold chill through Andy. Her long blonde hair—dirty and matted—covered her face, her attention on the ground.

Despite the close press of trees turning the dark shadows darker, the girl stood out as if tracked by a spotlight. The nearly full moon found a way through the canopy and lit her up. The glare of it highlighted the stains on her dirty nightie. A mild evening, but not so mild the kid wouldn't get hypothermia.

The girl continued to shuffle forwards. If the undergrowth tore at her pale and exposed legs like Andy would expect it to, she didn't show it. She must have heard his stopping, reversing, and now idling on the side of the road, but the child didn't look up once. The longer he watched her, the more details he noticed. She shivered, giving her progression the slightest of stutters. Her skin was so pale it proved tricky to know where her nightie ended and she began. Her pasty limbs were stick thin.

Could it be a ghost? Did ghosts feel the cold?

It could be stress making him see things. Hell, he nearly drove himself off the road a few seconds ago. Maybe something deep inside took over, saving his life by creating a girl who didn't exist.

Yes, that had to be it.

But Andy still remained on the side of the road and watched her. "I'm not going to kill myself now. You can take the kid away."

The car's only response came in the form of a ticking engine and blowing fans.

Andy picked his phone up, the glow of it bursting through the soft glow of his car's interior. The device buzzed, rejecting his sweaty thumbprint. He typed in his code: her date of birth.

Andy stared down at the contact. *Home.* Chesky would know what to do. But should he call her? She'd made it pretty clear. O-V-E-R didn't leave any room for confusion. He needed to stand on his own two feet. He needed to stop being so passive. Not one for friends, he didn't have anyone else to call. His mum would be in bed. Besides, only Chesky would take him seriously. Anyone else, including his mother, would assume he'd lost the plot. Had he?

"I'm imagining her," Andy said to the empty car. He banged the heel of his hand against his forehead. The girl continued to walk through the woods no more than ten metres away. "I'm imagining her. She's not real."

But she looked real, and anything could happen to her.

Could he drive away from that? Could he let someone's child die cold, scared, and alone because he had no backbone?

ANDY STARED AT HIS PHONE. CHESKY HAD ALWAYS BEEN A support to him, even over the past few years. He'd not given much back in that time. He'd not given much to anyone since it had happened. But she *would* know what to do.

After shaking his head, Andy put his phone down again. He should drive away. What kind of nutter got out of a car on a road like this and chased a figment of his imagination around a cold, dark, and damp woods? What if the police stopped? They'd have him committed and he'd lose his job. Homeless, jobless, and with no friends to help him out, he'd be sleeping on flattened boxes in a cold doorway by the end of the week.

But what if she was real? It kept coming back to that. What if she was real and he left her? Could he live with himself if he saw a missing persons ad with her small face on it? And then a report on the news of a body found in the woods? Could he really do what he always did? Fuck all. Less than fuck all. Since it had happened, he'd been nothing but a hindrance to anyone who'd had the misfortune of crossing his path.

Andy beeped the car's horn and jumped because of the blare.

A slow and unrelenting trudge, the girl continued forward. She could be real. She could be sleepwalking. She could be escaping someone. Someone who would find her if Andy didn't help.

But the sound of a horn would wake her, wouldn't it? Or at least attract her attention. Andy pressed the horn again. This time, he held it down for longer.

The ticking engine, the blow of the car's heaters, his own quickened breaths … but still nothing from the girl.

He should move on and act like he'd not seen her. He knew how to do nothing. Besides, people saw ghosts all the time. He didn't need to tell anyone about it. No one would believe him if he did.

Find a shitty hotel and get some sleep. It had been a long day. Tar pumped through his veins, fatigue creeping into his aching muscles. Tomorrow, once rested, he could ignore the reports of a missing girl if they came. Turn a blind eye to the articles that would follow the story until her body turned up. Change channels when the news played the money shot of the grieving parents. He could shut his ears to the stories of the unspeakable things done to her when the wrong people found her alone and defenceless. He could hear how wonderful she was … bright … promising … How she wouldn't have hurt a fly and a million other clichés that said nothing of the person-shaped hole in the lives of those who loved her. How she didn't deserve to die so young. How no one deserved to die so fucking young. Like he didn't know.

"But she doesn't exist," Andy said to the empty car. "She *doesn't* exist."

Andy pushed the clutch down and slipped the car into first gear.

"For fuck's sake." Andy put the car back into neutral before he turned the engine off. He opened the door, dragging the cool night air inside. "You'd best not be a fucking ghost, you little shit."

THE UNDERGROWTH SNAGGED AND TUGGED ON ANDY'S JEANS like he'd expected it to. God knew how she managed it in just a nightie. "Hey, you!" The heady smell of woodland decay hung ripe, stirred up by his clumsy steps. The boggy ground threatened to claim his shoes. The nearly full moon broke through the canopy, showing him a path while it kept her illuminated.

The girl stared at the ground and continued to shake. If she made a sound, the crunch of Andy's clumsy steps drowned it out. The closer he got to her, the less she looked like a ghost. "Girl! I—arghhh!" A barbed vine hooked into his cheek and dragged a streak of fire across his face. A bit too late now, but he still raised his forearms to prevent any more brambles doing the same. His pulse quickened, sweat lifting beneath his collar, and he fought to suppress his frustration. "Girl! Listen to me!"

Surrounded by trees and shadows, the moon might have lit a path for Andy, but it did little to reveal the details of his current environment. Anything could have been hiding in the gloom. Even more reason to get the girl out of there. Besides, he shouldn't be afraid of what he couldn't see. He'd left his fears of monsters beneath the bed and wardrobe trolls behind with pee-soaked mattresses and his four times table. She needed him. Nothing else mattered.

"I'm getting closer to you." Twigs and branches snapped, and wayward thorns remained in Andy's trousers, scratching his legs. An elephant would have tracked her with more grace, but as long as he caught up.

The closer Andy got to the girl, the more the moon failed him. Where it had been a spotlight, the clouds above first tinted the lens and now buried it. Good job she chose to wear white. He kept his focus on the child. To take in the encroaching hostility surrounding him would rob him of his forward momentum.

No more than two metres between them now. "Hey, little girl, what's going on? Why are you out here?"

A metre and a half away, his torso itched with sweat. "Where are your parents?"

The girl stopped. Andy halted too, deafened by the pant of his own quickened breaths. It had been a long time since he'd done any physical exercise. Trudging through life had been enough of a challenge over the past three years; now he couldn't even climb a set of stairs without getting breathless. He shook with adrenaline, his legs buzzing from the fresh cuts

After about thirty seconds, Andy stepped closer. No more than a metre separated them. "Girl, where are your parents?"

Filthy hair, her nightie covered in dirt and filled with holes. Her skin so pale, she looked starved of vitamin D. Like she'd spent her life living underground. She kept her face hidden. Now she'd stopped, she shook more than ever. He needed to get her into the warm car and take her to the police.

Close enough to reach out and touch her, Andy kept his hands at his sides. "Excuse me, why are you out here? What's going on?"

Andy took slow steps, walking around so he stood in front of her, expecting her to burst to life at any moment. He hunched down and placed a hand on one of her folded arms, fighting the urge to withdraw at the icy touch of her skin. As dirty from the front, her matted hair hung in filthy dreadlocks.

Slowly, the girl lifted her head, her long blonde hair parting to reveal her small face. A button nose, cracked lips, and bright blue eyes. Thick white strips sat beneath her irises as if the weight of her woes dragged on the lower half of her face. She shook her head, her quiet voice croaky like she hadn't used it for the longest time. "I wish you hadn't followed me."

ANDY'S BRAIN THROBBED, STINGING WITH EVERY BEAT OF HIS

pulse as if it had swollen to be too large for his skull. His eyes were ready to crack and run down his cheeks like egg yolk. And he welcomed it. He'd go blind to stop the pain. While lying in the foetal position, he held his forehead and squinted to take in his poorly lit surroundings. But even the gloomy environment stung his eyes.

When the pain eased a little, he gasped. He'd best make the most of the respite between the paralysing waves. Several blinks helped Andy piece together his surroundings. He shivered, the cold from the stone floor permeating his body.

Andy fought against his dizziness and slowly sat up. A hand against the damp wall—the sandstone leaving cold grit against his palm—he waited for everything to settle down. Whatever they'd injected him with, it still ran through his system. His head spun and nausea clamped his stomach. He shot out a weak cough to try to clear the burn of bile on the back of his throat.

As Andy's consciousness returned, another pain surfaced. Like his headache, it throbbed in time with his pulse. With anything a few metres outside his field of vision still blurred, he looked down at his right thigh, frowning as if it would help him understand his situation. They'd cut the leg from his jeans, and a white bandage had been wrapped from his knee to his groin. A dinner-plate-sized bloodstain glistened on the fabric.

He drew a sharp breath through clenched teeth, his stomach plummeting. Despite the deep sting, whatever they'd injected him with took the edge off the agony. God help him when it wore off.

Andy's sight had cleared enough to reveal a barred door locking him in the small room. The glint of a new padlock subdued any thought of escape. A small wooden bench sat at the other end against the far wall. It looked like the room hadn't been used in years. More a dungeon than a prison cell, the place belonged in the dark ages.

A tiny window above the bench let in a small amount of light from the bright moon. Andy trembled as he got to his feet and shuffled to the back of his cell. The window sat in a crumbling wooden frame that had bloated with damp. One hard whack would drive the glass and frame clear of the hole. For what good it would do; they'd have to cut a lot more of him away before he'd fit through a gap that small.

His vision improving, Andy looked back at the barred door. A walkway separated him and another locked cell. It had someone inside, hidden in the shadows. He hobbled across the small space, leaned against the cold bars keeping him locked in, and gasped. A prisoner like him, the small girl from the woods stared straight back. "You bitch," he hissed. "*You* did this to me."

The same listless and sunken eyes he'd seen in the woods, the girl's jaw worked like a cow's. Dirt stained her pale skin, and blood coated her maw. The same white bands of depression lit up the bottom of her blue irises.

When she lifted something to her mouth and took a bite, the air left Andy's lungs. Her small hand clung onto a clump of raw meat. The pain in his thigh flared up again and it took him a few seconds to find his words. "Are you eating *me*?"

THE SLAPPING OF THE GIRL'S LIPS FILLED THE SILENCE BETWEEN the two cells. She chewed then swallowed before taking another bite from the small chunk of flesh. Every wet squelch twisted Andy's stomach. The desire to scream at her ran tension through his body, tightening every fibre of his being. Yet he stood there transfixed, captivated by her blank expression.

Had she not already spoken to him in the woods, Andy

would have assumed she couldn't. Very few synapses appeared to be firing behind her glazed stare. "What is this place?"

The girl looked to her left, and Andy followed her line of sight. The dirty corridor between them ended with a set of stone stairs leading out of their basement dungeon. "I don't know where we are."

Andy jumped back from the girl's words, his thigh sending a searing warning that he shouldn't try such sharp movements a second time.

"We move from place to place," she said, "and never stay anywhere long. We need to keep ahead of the police."

Maybe the sudden movement had made it worse, or maybe the anaesthetic had started to wear off; either way, the deep throb in Andy's thigh ran even deeper as if straight to the bone. He pushed his words out. "What are they going to do with me?"

The girl took another bite of his thigh and chewed.

"Stupid question, I suppose."

No matter what she said, the girl delivered it with the same monotone, her features fixed as if the muscles animating her face had shut down. "You don't have long left. Now we've started, we'll eat you in the next few days."

"Who are *we*?"

For the first time, the girl's face changed, her eyes widening ever so slightly. "Bad people. *Very* bad people."

"How did you end up with them?"

"They aren't all bad. They used to have a nice lady."

"Huh?"

"She taught me everything. She learned me to speak. She said I was born, but no one ever knew I was born."

"You weren't born in a hospital?"

"No hospital."

"And you didn't go to school?"

"No school. Just here. With them."

"The bad people?"

"Apart from the nice lady."

"So the authorities don't know you exist?"

"Authorities?"

"What happened to the nice lady?"

"She's gone. Gone the same way everyone goes. Gone the same way you'll go." The girl dropped her attention to Andy's bandaged thigh and wetted her lips with the tip of her tongue. Her cheeks were hollow, her face withdrawn. From the look of her wiry arms and legs, were she naked at that moment, Andy was sure he'd see every bone in her body.

"You ate her too?"

The girl dropped her gaze to the floor while Andy tightened his grip on the cold bars. The shiny padlock glinted in the weak light. His head spun and the bandage grew damper with every passing second. If he didn't hold on, he'd crumple where he stood. After a few seconds of waiting for the girl to look up, he released a hard sigh, shook his head, and said, "My god."

IF SHE SPOKE THE TRUTH, AND ANDY CERTAINLY BELIEVED SHE spoke the truth, then she didn't know any better. A child raised to be a cannibal couldn't be blamed for their actions, as abhorrent as they were. Beautiful blue eyes, long blonde hair, delicate features. She couldn't have been any older than about ten. Too young to know any different. He should focus on that rather than the horrific experience of watching someone eat him. "What's your name?"

"They call me Worm."

"*Worm?*"

Again, she responded as if she had no attachment to the words. "They say they go fishing with me. I'm the worm. The bait. They make me walk through dark places in the middle of the night. *Scary* places. Although I quite like them because it means I get out. One day I'm going to run. The kind lady said I should. She said as soon as I get a chance, I should run like the wind."

"So why haven't you?"

"They heard her."

"And that's why they killed her?"

A tilt of her head to one side, the girl said, "Yes."

"And you don't have a real name?"

"Worm."

The rattle of a freeing padlock silenced them. The shadow at the top of the stairs made it impossible to see what came their way as the hinges on the old wooden door creaked.

ANDY STEPPED BACK INTO THE SHADOWS, LEANED AGAINST THE sandstone wall, and slid down it to the cold and hard floor. He rolled over into the foetal position, lying on a gritty layer of chipped stone and dirt. He shuffled once or twice before the searing burn in his thigh pulled his attention away from the mild discomfort beneath him.

The angry incessant buzz in Andy's leg grew worse as footsteps descended the stone stairs. It dared him to move. Just the smallest shift to ease his pain. But they were too close. Better they believed him to still be unconscious.

The steps continued with a slow and deliberate purpose. They taunted Andy, daring him to look. His back to the cell door, he pressed his eyes closed and did what he did best: he lay down, ready to take whatever came his way. No wonder Chesky had ended it. How could she love such a passive wimp?

The footsteps reached the bottom of the stone stairs and

walked along the narrow corridor. Each click of a heel against the hard floor chipped away at Andy's resolve, daring him to look. Just once. They wouldn't notice.

Andy suppressed a flinch when keys rattled directly outside his cell. The click of the released padlock and then a yawn from the opening metal door followed.

Grit popped beneath each step as the person moved to within a metre of Andy. They breathed heavily as if the small walk to check on him had taken its toll.

Relaxing the tight squeeze on his eyes as the boots walked around in front of him, Andy fought to maintain his even breaths. The rich scent of damp boot leather just millimetres from his face, they'd shatter his nose with one hard kick.

The person lifted the foot closest to him. The cold, hard press of a gritty sole pushed into his right cheek. But he remained passive and kept his focus on the sensation in his thigh. Although the person leaned some of their weight against Andy's face, they halted before the pain made him yell.

The pressure lifted and Andy focused on his breaths. In and out, in and out. Slow and measured like that of someone who'd been drugged.

The footsteps retraced their gritty path from his cell. Andy anticipated the slamming door and resisted his need to flinch as the mocking metallic cackle tore through the building beyond. After the click of the padlock being resecured, the steps walked away and ascended the stairs.

A baritone voice yelling through the building beyond confirmed it to be a man. "He's still out. I'll check on him again later."

When Andy finally opened his eyes, long after the door at the top of the stairs had been shut and locked, he rolled over and gasped to find the girl fixed on him. "They prefer to eat people when they're alive," she said. Hunger burned as the only glow in her bland stare. Maybe she preferred it too. "They often take a sample." She licked her cracked lips. "But then they hold out. It excites them for what's to come. They say meat tastes much better if you're listening to it scream."

ANDY DIDN'T KNOW HOW MUCH TIME HAD PASSED SINCE THE girl revealed his fate. Eaten alive. If there was an appropriate response, he hadn't yet found it. Besides, he had more immediate concerns. Every time it felt like the anaesthetic had worn off, the burn in his thigh rose to an entirely new level, a molten spear being pressed deeper into his leg with every fresh wave.

While Andy rode out the agony—his brow sodden with sweat—the girl said, "Do you have any children?"

She'd lusted after his living flesh and now she wanted to make small talk? What did she want to do next, discuss the weather? Make a joke about two buses turning up at once?

After about thirty seconds, the girl asked again, "Do you have any children?"

"So I'm lying here, waiting for them to eat me alive— waiting for *you* to eat me alive—and you're asking me about my family?"

The same detached stare regarded him.

"Okay, fine," he said. "*No*, I don't have any children."

The padlock on the door at the top of the stairs snapped open again, cutting their conversation short.

MAYBE THE SAME PERSON WHO VISITED HIM THE LAST TIME, maybe not. Either way, they followed the same routine: entering

Andy's cell before pressing the cold, hard, and gritty sole of their boot against his face.

Like before, Andy lay there, tolerating the sting from the boot against one cheek, and the sting from the cold concrete against the other.

ONCE THE GUARD LEFT, ANDY SAT UP SLOWLY. THE LITTLE GIRL continued to stare at him. "My wife and I have just split up. I don't know why I'm telling you this, but I was thinking about killing myself when I saw you in the woods. I was driving towards a row of trees with my seatbelt off. I feel like I made the wrong decision."

"Why would you kill yourself?"

Not only did Andy have a thousand fire ants feasting on his thigh, but his hips ached from sitting on the hard floor. He rocked from side to side in an attempt to find some relief. "Life got too hard." When he looked at the girl, he laughed. "Probably difficult for you to understand, right? I mean, look at the fucking life you've had to live. How can I say my life's shit?"

The girl's expression remained blank. She couldn't have been any older than ten, but she had a resilience in her maudlin stance that would take Andy a century or more to develop. His pasty and pale frame, his pudgy hands, his apathy for life when it got hard. How pathetic. She'd experienced things he couldn't even comprehend. "You know what?" he said. "I'm not going to lie down and take this anymore. We need to get you out of here."

The same cold stare. The same sunken eyes. The same pale skin. The same monotone voice. "They told me if I ever escape to get help, that I'll get in trouble too. I'm one of them. I eat people like they do. I'm evil like they are. Evil people get punished."

"They're full of shit. None of this is your fault." While pointing at the small window in the far wall of his cell, the dull glow from the moon shining in on them, Andy said, "The people out there will help you, and I'll make sure you get to them."

NOW ANDY HAD PROMISED HE'D FREE THE GIRL, HE HAD TO come up with a way to do it. For the past ten minutes or so, they hadn't spoken while he looked at the same three walls and the same locked door. Even in the shadows of the basement, the large shiny padlock winked at him. It mocked his ideas before they had a chance to form. Not only did he need to work out how to get out of there, but he had plenty of questions for the girl too. But how could he ask them? *What do people taste like? What do I taste like? Had they done anything else horrible to her? Who was her mum? The kind lady?*

"What happened to you?" the girl asked.

For the past three years, a lump had sat in Andy's throat. Some days it resided as no more than a minor irritation, although maybe not for those around him; Chesky used to snap at how often he coughed. Some days it swelled to the point where it damn near suffocated him. The lump engorged at that one simple question, breaking his voice. "What do you mean?"

If she'd blinked at any point, Andy hadn't witnessed it. She continued her monotone line of enquiry. Curious, not concerned. Did she have concern in her? "You're not telling me something."

Andy winced and dragged another breath in through his

clenched teeth. He rocked where he sat to try to ease the pain in his hips. Not that it needed easing. And truth be told, it would take a lot more than wriggling to escape his permanent discomfort. Everything he'd tried over the past three years had failed. "She was called Gwen." It had taken the detached questioning from a girl he didn't know to get the words out. If only he'd let Chesky help when she'd offered. He would never have left the house that night.

Although surrounded by darkness, the girl's pale skin, soiled shirt, and white strips beneath her sad eyes caught the moonlight. For the first time, her eyebrows lifted as if she felt something.

"She was my daughter."

"What happened to her?"

"Hodgkin's lymphoma."

"What's that?"

A raging torrent slammed into him, damn near throwing him back to the cold floor. Andy took several breaths and focused on the red bandage swaddling his thigh. His eyes burned, his breathing obscured by the lump in his throat. "Cancer. Some even refer to it as *curable* cancer. Well, you know what?"

"It wasn't?"

A deep sigh, and Andy dropped his head. He lost control of his buckling bottom lip. "No."

"I'm so sorry."

Like with her raised eyebrows, sorrow sat in her eyes. Like he'd done a thousand times already with colleagues and neighbours, Andy opened his mouth to tell her it was fine. To make her feel better about his grief. But he stopped himself. Why should he take her gesture away from her, and why should he try to make her feel okay about it? "Thank you. She was about your age when she died."

A rattle of keys called down to them. A second later, the lock on the door at the top of the stairs snapped open.

ANOTHER PRESS OF ANOTHER COLD AND DIRTY BOOT. THE added pressure spoke of their impatience. His face sandwiched between hard leather and the gritty floor, Andy felt the stinging tear of his skin splitting beneath the twist of their sole. What would they do next time? Would there even be a next time? They had to run out of patience sooner or later.

Andy grabbed the guard's ankle, lifting their foot from his face as he jumped to life. He grabbed the ankle of their standing leg and yanked hard.

The sudden movement sent electric tendrils streaking down his exposed right thigh and into his groin. But not even the burn of an opening wound could slow him down. As the guard landed on their back, he crawled on top of them and punched them on the nose.

The moonlight revealed the face of a woman. What the fuck was he doing? He'd never hit a woman in his life. But she wanted to eat him. She'd kept a child imprisoned. He drove a hard punch into the centre of her face, turning her instantly limp. Goosebumps from head to toe, the adrenaline lighting him up, he punched her again, her head snapping from side to side with each blow.

By the time Andy stopped, his hands throbbed almost as much as his thigh. The woman's face a pulped mess, her eyes swollen shut, her mouth and maw coated in her own blood.

The same cold assessment of his actions stared at Andy from the cell opposite. He spoke to her through heavy breaths. "I'm going to get us out of here. You need to do as I say, okay?"

The girl nodded.

ANDY SEARCHED THE UNCONSCIOUS GUARD'S POCKETS. SHE only had two keys on her. He took them both. Half her body lay out in the corridor from where she'd fallen through the doorway, so he grabbed her ankles and dragged her in, limping because of his wound.

Once he'd pulled the guard fully into the cell, he leaned close to her swollen and bloody face. The slight rattle of laboured respiration drove the subtle rise and fall of her chest. Wincing while he straightened again, he pushed the sole of his left shoe into her cheek. He ground the grit into her skin with a hard twist.

By the time Andy pulled his foot away, blood from the freshly opened wound ran into her already coated maw. If they'd have pushed that hard on him, he would have flinched. She must be unconscious. He left her in the cell.

Half an eye on the open door at the top of the stairs and the deep shadows beyond, Andy's hands shook as he slowly closed his cell door and clicked the padlock shut. A dry mouth and rapid pulse. If they found him, he'd be screwed.

The sounds of movement called down the stairs at Andy from somewhere within the building, but nothing emerged from the shadows, and the silence resumed.

A small window like the one in Andy's cell sat in the wall on his left. About five feet from the floor, it too had a bloated and crumbling wooden frame. Despite being covered in dirt, the moonlight made it mildly transparent. He'd assumed they were in a basement. The grass on the other side of the window confirmed it.

The girl's attention on him the entire time, Andy said, "We're going to get out of here, okay?"

The girl nodded.

"Whatever's waiting for us up there, I'll make sure we get through it. You just need to listen to me. Are you ready for this?"

The girl nodded again.

The window in the corridor let in a bar of moonlight. When Andy held the two keys in it, his stomach sank. The padlocks on his cell and the girl's were similar. The two keys were wildly different. The key that had opened Andy's cell fitted the girl's padlock but wouldn't unlock it. He couldn't get the other key in the hole. All the while, the girl's detached stare remained on him. Now he'd moved closer, he had to ruffle his nose against her dirty stench.

A shrug of her shoulders, and the girl said, "Thanks for trying anyway."

"What do you mean?"

"Well, once you're up there and have a chance at freedom, you won't come back for me. Why would you?"

Although Andy opened his mouth, she cut him off. "I don't blame you. They want to eat you. *I* want to eat you. You should get out of here as soon as you can."

Such a clear understanding from someone so young and seemingly detached. "Who's most likely to have your keys?"

"They call her Nell." A twist of something ran across her face. Revulsion? Fear? Hard to tell.

"What does she look like?"

The girl damn near spat every word. "She's *skinny* and tall. She has red hair and a *mean* face. A mean, *mean* face."

"I'm going to get you out of here. Even if it kills me."

The girl reverted to monotone. "It might."

It had been a long time since Andy considered himself

fit, but even he would have expected to make it farther up the flight of stairs than four steps. Hot and cold waves emanated from the wound in his thigh. He gritted his teeth and tried to ride it out. After wiping his sweat-dampened brow, he waited for the knot in his stomach to loosen before he pushed on. How the hell did he expect to find the key and liberate the girl in this state?

But the hows didn't matter. Whatever happened, the kid needed a life, and someone needed to give it to her. He'd watched one taken away from his little girl. Nothing would bring Gwen back, but he had more motivation than most to make sure the tiny prisoner got the freedom she deserved.

Andy pushed on up the worn stairs, his exposed right leg turning numb with the cold. The sharper pieces of grit bit into the bare sole of his right foot.

Every inhale dragged the damp and wretched atmosphere into Andy's lungs, the heavy air adding to his struggles as he puffed like an old chain-smoker.

Two more wobbly steps and Andy made it to the top. He leaned against the wall to let his balance reset and his breathing level. Eight stairs and he'd come close to being defeated already. Whatever resolve he had in him, he'd best find it soon.

Thankfully, the female guard had left the door open when she came down. He didn't need the groaning hinges announcing his movements to the building's ravenous residents.

A narrow windowless corridor about three metres long separated Andy and the next room. A small wash of moonlight revealed rusted bed frames lining either side of what must have once been a large ward. The place had clearly been abandoned for decades.

Andy moved on but halted after two steps. He leaned against the wall again, fighting the resistance in his tight chest. The darkness had hidden the twenty or so bodies when he'd been farther back. They lay on the floor and sang a chorus of deep breaths, one or two issuing low snores.

When Andy stepped closer, a sharp piece of stone dug into his bare right foot. An involuntary reaction, he lifted it, the wound on his thigh running molten rods straight to his groin.

Several seconds passed where Andy clenched his jaw and breathed through his nose. The sleepers in the room appeared to still be unconscious. At least he hadn't stood on glass. Although, with the state of the place, surely it would just be a matter of time. The girl had told him they moved around a lot, so why would they bother cleaning anywhere if they didn't plan on staying? Eat someone and move on. The longer he lingered in the corridor, the more chance someone would wake up, so he set off towards the doorway leading into the next room. He needed to find the woman with the keys to the girl's cell.

A groan halted Andy. While holding his breath, he ignored his buzzing thigh's demand for attention and listened. It came from somewhere deep in the building. Did they have another victim? But as he listened to it, he shook his head. Not a victim. It was the sound of people fucking.

Andy poked his head into the grotty ward. The collective stench of the filthy bodies lifted a gag into the bottom of his throat, but he swallowed it back. A carpet of sleeping cannibals between him and freedom. Had the girl been correct in her assessment of what he'd do? If he got past them, would it be the wisest thing to go back? Maybe it would be easier to call the police. But what if they noticed he'd gone and moved on before the police arrived? What then for the child? If he did nothing else in this life, he had to help her. And maybe with the guards either asleep or distracted, there wouldn't be a better time.

If he didn't move now, he never would, so Andy kept his back to the damp wall and shuffled into the room.

THE STONE FLOOR CONTINUED FROM THE CORRIDOR THROUGH the room with the sleeping bodies. As if having a numb foot didn't serve as a potent enough reminder of his missing right shoe, Andy also had to contend with the sting of standing on small pieces of brick and stone. Limping because of his thigh, he skirted around the edge of the ward.

Now he'd fully entered the room, the stench of dirt, sweat, and flatulence assaulted Andy from all sides. He screwed his face up and pushed on, moving down the walkway in the middle like a baby wildebeest through a gang of sleeping crocodiles. Should even one of them wake up ... Meat tasted so much better when it screamed.

The poor light made it harder to see, but Andy hadn't yet passed the woman the girl described. Red hair, skinny, and tall ... maybe she even had a mean face when sleeping. Men, women, and a couple of teenagers, but not the key holder. Not yet.

Despite the snores and snorts around him, the slap of flesh and grunts of exertion continued to call to Andy from somewhere else in the building. It sounded like rutting pigs.

About halfway across the ward, Andy took a break to slow his breaths. Not heavy yet, but if he wanted to maintain his stealth, he needed a short pause. If the sleepers woke up, he wouldn't stand a chance. The muggy air added to the dryness in his throat, and when he gulped, it dragged an itch down to the permanent lump. The need to cough crawled like a live bug, the tiny legs irritating his oesophagus.

When Andy reached the doorway out of the ward, he heaved a relieved sigh. Not that he'd achieved much. None of the sleepers were the woman he needed, and he'd have to walk back through there to help the girl later.

Floorboards lined the hallway between Andy and the sounds of pleasure in the room opposite. The long corridor stretched both ways. The shadows on his left turned pitch black after no more than a few metres. Right led to a doorless exit to thick woodland. But he couldn't leave the girl. One of the fuckers sounded female. Hopefully Nell. He had to check it out.

The glow of a small flame shone in the room. Both ways seemed clear, so Andy crossed the hallway, fighting against his instinct to run right.

A single candle glowed in the far corner of the room, glistening off the naked sweating bodies of one woman and two men. Or nearly naked. The man attached to the back of the woman still wore his boots and socks. The woman on all fours between them had red hair, skinny hips, and sagging breasts. Even now, her face had a sharp twist of cruelty. Outnumbered, but in this trio she clearly called the shots despite her position of subservience. It had to be Nell.

A pile of clothes lay between Andy and the three fuckers. The candlelight might have been weak, but the large bulge in the pocket of one of the pairs of trousers had to be the keys. As if aiding him, the flame on the candle swelled and caught the glint of a key ring.

A snort from the room behind him sent a surge through Andy's heart. He pulled back into the hallway and faced the ward. A woman shifted on the floor, snorted again, and then rolled over onto her side before she fell back into the rhythm of sleep. The slapping of flesh and deep groans continued in the candlelit room, oblivious to anything but sating carnal desire.

Unless the man behind Nell turned around, he wouldn't see Andy. The one who could seemed more concerned with the grip he had on the back of Nell's head. Maybe a better chance would come up and maybe it wouldn't, but Andy didn't have the time to wait.

In spite of the candle's best efforts, shadows lay against the walls and in the corners of the room. Darkness oozed from the very fabric of the building, and one candle could only do so much. Andy slipped inside and leaned against the damp brick. He skirted around the edge of the room, his eyes stinging from where he refused to blink.

The deeper Andy moved into the room, the thicker the dirty funk of sex. Not only did they fuck like pigs, but they smelled like them too. It had clearly been a long time since any of this lot had washed.

Close to the trousers, Andy bit his bottom lip as he leaned down to grab them. He held his breath while dragging the keys from the woman's pocket. They came free with little resistance, the dull light glinting off them.

Andy closed his palm around the cold metal while holding his breath. It left him a moment later in a gasp when he looked up. The man at the front of the woman—the man having his dick sucked—now stared straight at him.

THE KEYS STUNG ANDY'S TIGHTENING GRIP AS HE STOOD pinned in the spotlight of the man's gaze. A slight twist of pleasure teased the edges of the man's mouth. Somewhere between orgasm and rage. Either way, he looked set to erupt.

Andy's heart damn near burst and his already dry throat turned arid. If it came to a footrace, they'd be on him before he reached the hallway. But could he really fight them? What other choice did he have? A breath to settle himself, he arranged several keys so they poked from his right fist. Better to fight than get chased down like a wounded fox.

At the man's mercy, Andy waited.

But then the man dropped his attention to the back of Nell's bobbing head before releasing a deep groan and running his fingers through her matted ginger hair.

Andy shifted a step towards the hallway despite now being closer to a doorway leading deeper into the building. A new angle, only slightly different, but enough to show him the light reflecting off the milky layer covering the man's eyes. He let go of the hard twist gripping his upper body. The man was blind.

After another step, Andy froze again, a line of chilled gooseflesh streaking up his back.

A woman's voice this time, it rang through the abandoned institution. It came from the downstairs basement and had the nasal ring of someone who'd had their face smashed in. "The prisoner's gone missing," she shrieked. "He's *escaped!*"

THE FUCKERS STOPPED FUCKING, ANDY'S STOMACH FLIPPING AS the man behind Nell withdrew with a wet squelch.

Nell might have been skinny, but when upright she stood over six feet tall, the long stretch of her pasty back covered in a sweaty sheen. Despite her narrow hips, her wide shoulders made her triangular. Her large hands would ball into deadly fists. Before she and the other man turned around, Andy darted for the door closest to him.

Dark like every other part of the decrepit building, the abandoned room had the same damp smell, although this time it was tinged with rusted metal and rotten wood. Better than the festering soup stirred up by the threesome. He slipped the keys into his pocket. The little girl would have to wait.

The hard bare walls and empty room threw the sound of Andy's breathing back at him as if mocking his panic. The shadows gave no suggestions as to where he should hide, and the woman's voice rang through the building again. "The prisoner's escaped. We need to wake the fuck up."

Nell's voice thrummed with a gravelled snarl. "Shit! Where do you think he's gone?"

For the next few seconds, Andy spun on the spot. Then he looked up. The ceiling had a hole in it. But how the hell would he get up there?

Barely able to stand, he had no chance of jumping.

Fortunately, Nell went towards the sound, charging into the ward where everyone slept while issuing a barking alarm. "Wake up! Wake up!"

It had given Andy a few extra seconds. Hopefully he could make them count.

THE ONLY LIGHT IN THE GLOOMY ROOM CAME FROM THE CANDLE next door. It offered a narrow corridor of vision, hiding the chest of drawers in the corner until Andy damn near fell over them. About a metre tall and three metres wide, he tugged on them and they shook as if one hard kick would turn them to dust. But the sleepers in the ward were mobilising, Nell still shouting for them to get up. If there were any better or more immediate options, he hadn't found them.

Andy bit down on his bottom lip as if it would somehow mute the screech of wood across stone while Nell continued to shout two rooms away.

The chest of drawers in place, Andy pushed out a hard exhale as he raised his left foot. When he'd lifted it about thirty centimetres from the floor, his standing leg failed him. He hit the hard and dirty stone, his thigh flexing, ripping his wound wider. Sweat instantly covered his body like he had a fever. Tears itched his eyes and his vision blurred. He couldn't do it.

But when the galloping footsteps left the ward and burst out into the corridor he'd just crossed, he gritted his teeth and pulled himself up by the wobbly drawers.

All upper body strength, Andy pressed down on the drawers so he could first drag his good knee onto them and then use the strength in that leg to pull his weakened one up after. The footsteps spoke of the sleepers spreading out. Several of them beat a tattoo against wooden stairs somewhere in the building.

Just standing up on the old piece of furniture challenged the strength of Andy's right leg, the wooden structure creaking as it swayed beneath him.

The hole had once been a loft hatch. It had been hard to tell from the floor because the edges were jagged with decay. Andy reached up, grabbed a bar of wood and tugged on it. Swollen with damp like the window frame in his cell, it disintegrated in his grip. "Fuck it."

Footsteps headed Andy's way. At least three people entered the room Nell and her two lovers had been in. He grunted as he jumped at the hatch and reached into the loft, the drawers falling on their side when he boosted from them.

Andy reached into the darkness but found nothing to cling on to and slid backwards, a moment of weightlessness lifting his heart into his throat. Just before he fell, his hands hooked over a beam, the strong bar of wood halting his fall.

Andy pulled his left leg into the loft and rested his knee against the frame before dragging his right in after it. He bit back a scream as his thigh scraped over the jagged wood on its way in. The second he got clear, several people entered the room.

S<small>ITTING</small> <small>JUST</small> <small>OUT</small> <small>OF</small> <small>SIGHT</small> <small>OF</small> <small>THE</small> <small>ROOM</small> <small>BELOW</small>, A<small>NDY</small>

perched on the beam he'd used to drag himself up by, his right leg stretched out in front of him, his right fist balled waiting for the first head to poke up through the hole. Whack-a-mole for real. Crack-a-skull.

Darker than any part of the building Andy had been in so far, the space existed between floors. Thunder hammered above him from the search party who'd run upstairs. He leaned closer to the hatch and tracked the movement of those who'd entered the room by their steps. Surely the chest of drawers on their side would give him away.

A man's voice said, "There's no one here. Come on, we need to find that fucker."

Once they'd left the room, Andy stood up and paused. Had they really gone? A silent answer met his silent question, so he moved deeper into the loft space. He had just about enough room to walk with a hunch, the pressure of his crouch running straight to his thigh. Dustier than any other space he'd been in, it left a fuzzy layer against his teeth.

ANDY'S EYES ADJUSTED TO THE MURKY SPACE. THE ROOMS below had seemed dark when he'd passed through them, but they were lighter than the loft. They revealed themselves through the holes in their ceilings as dull glows punching up into the dusty space. It gave him a measure of the ground floor's footprint. The loft sat above at least six rooms. They wouldn't take long to search, and then what? Could he do anything but wait? Or should he move now? The cannibals were stretched thin because of their hasty search, would now be the best time to free the girl?

While moving over the beams with a stoop, Andy peered into the rooms below through the cracks. Slow progress, he pressed down on a beam with his leading foot, testing its ability to hold him before moving on to the next. Some were softer than others, but they all held. So far.

As he passed over the room that had hosted the grotesque threesome, Andy stopped. A crowd had gathered in there. A small hole, it showed about six of them, but there were more he couldn't see. The candlelight cast shadows across Nell's bitter face.

"We should check the woods," she said. "He must have gone out there."

A man shook his head. "But where would he go? There's nothing around for miles."

Nell lunged at the man, halting an inch from his face. "There are fucking trees out there and it's dark. It's the obvious place to hide, you *moron*."

A scalded puppy, the man pulled into himself and backed away.

"And if we don't find him," Nell said, stalking her pathetic victim, "we're going to need to find some other flesh to eat."

"What about the girl?"

Andy winced at the *crack* of Nell's open palm connecting with the side of the man's face, knocking him to the floor. She leaned over him. "You mention the girl again and I *promise* we'll eat you next whether we find the man or not."

The rest of the group closed in around the downed cannibal, some of them licking their lips. Like a pack of well-trained dogs, they needed just one word.

It wouldn't do any good to sit and watch degenerates argue with one another. Regardless of what happened to the man, they wouldn't forget about Andy. If he got away, their secret would be out.

What Andy had assumed to be the entirety of the ground floor when he'd climbed into the loft, he now saw differently.

The space doglegged, running over several more rooms. At the far end sat a small round window in an external wall.

Just as Andy pushed off, he stopped again when Nell said, "Let's do one more sweep of the building before we go outside."

Footsteps raced away from the woman in every direction, and Andy set off towards the small window. At some point, someone would check the loft.

Autumn wafted in through the round hole where there had once been glass, and Andy took a moment to breathe the cleaner air. It quelled his need to cough. Footsteps slammed above him, and although he didn't have to be silent, the wrong sound at the wrong time could easily give him away.

Andy poked his head outside. The ground about three metres below was covered in a bed of fallen leaves. It should soften the fall, and if he made it, he only had a short sprint to the thick woodland.

No way could he save the girl on his own. What could one crippled man do against a small army? The sooner he accepted that, the sooner he could get help for both of them.

Several people entered the room beneath him. The holes in the ceiling revealed their bats, knives, and clubs. Andy's heart skipped as the woman he'd locked in the cell followed the pack, a short metal bar in her grip.

How much longer before they were all outside? "I'm sorry, little girl," Andy muttered as he hung his bad leg out first, the air cool against his exposed skin. The keys in his pocket jabbed into his good thigh as if reminding him of their presence. But he couldn't help her if he didn't save himself.

MAYBE ANDY HAD IMAGINED THE VOICE OF HIS DAUGHTER.

She'd burst into his mind a lot in the past three years. Usually, she offered words of comfort. Words of support. And sometimes a berating at the state of things between him and Chesky. But she'd never been so assertive before. The one word shattered through his psyche like a thunderclap. *No!*

Andy pulled his leg back into the loft. An imagining of his daughter or his conscience, it didn't matter, he couldn't leave the girl with these people. More of them had gathered in the room below, their weapons increasingly inventive. Hammers, spanners, and one of them had a wood saw, the blade either rusty with time or coated in dried blood.

"This search is pointless," one of them said. "He's in the woods."

The woman Andy had locked in the cell nodded. "I think so too. Why would he stay in here?"

"We should get out there sooner rather than later. We can tell Nell there's nowhere else to look. The longer we wait, the more of a head start he'll have."

None of them replied. They didn't need to. The silence said it all. *Go on then. You tell Nell!*

Andy reached up and found a beam to lean against. It took some of the strain off his legs.

The heavy steps of the tall woman then entered the room, and the same voice that had spoken a moment ago addressed her with a stammer. "H-h-he's not in here. We need to plan how we're going to search the woods."

The silence lasted so long Andy shifted over to another gap. A hard frown dominated Nell's face and she worked her jaw as if chewing her words to a pulp before she spat them at him.

The man clearly couldn't take it anymore and filled the loaded silence. "Or … or … or you decide what we should do."

Nell's voice snapped through the abandoned building. "Everyone! Here now!"

If Andy wanted a better moment than this, he could be waiting a long time. The collective thunder of the cannibals closed in from all over the building. Wincing with every step as the wound on his thigh opened and closed, he made his return journey across the loft. Splinters from the beams sank into the sole of his exposed right foot.

THE CANNIBALS WERE YET TO LEAVE. JUST TWO ROOMS AWAY, but at least they were all together. Andy slipped from the loft hatch and dropped to the floor. His legs failed him.

A moment or two to breathe through the worst of it, Andy then scrambled to his feet. If he lay there too long, they'd find him and overwhelm him like rats on an injured dog. They tasted better when they screamed.

Riding out the sting in his thigh with heavy breathing, Andy listened to the voices two rooms away. They continued to discuss their plan for searching the woods.

Where Andy had limped before, the fall and a foot filled with splinters damn near robbed him of his ability to remain upright. His right hand against the closest wall for support, he shuffled through the first room into Nell's candlelit boudoir.

Maybe Andy imagined it, but as he moved through the fucking room, the smell of dirt and sex still perfumed the dank air. Almost as if the porous walls had sucked in the stench.

The cannibals continued their meeting next door. A thick brick wall separated them, so Andy focused on the ward opposite.

The shadows in the building had been Andy's friend all along. Cloaked by them once again, he poked his head out into the hallway. Shadows to his right. An open doorway out of there to his left.

Before the lure of the exit intensified, Andy hobbled across the floorboards in the direction of the ward.

Darker than the other rooms, Andy had been too focused on the sleeping cannibals the first time around to see why. Sheets had been pinned up over the windows to block out the light. The voices behind him grew distant as he shuffled towards the entrance to the cellar.

The door remained open. They must have assumed he wouldn't be back. Anyone in their right mind would have made a run for it. Andy descended the worn stone stairs. His cell hung wide. The remains of the broken padlock lay on the floor in front of it. Harder to tell from the distance, but it sounded like the cannibals were yet to move.

At the bottom of the stairs, panting, his throat swollen and dry, Andy tapped the bulge of keys in his pocket. Nell either hadn't noticed they'd gone, or she didn't realise he'd taken them. Otherwise, she would have been guarding the girl.

The girl's cage remained locked, and it took Andy a few seconds to find her in the gloom. She sat against the far wall, only her hollow glaze visible in the shadows.

Andy swallowed. "I told you I'd be back."

If she felt anything about what he'd just said, she didn't show it.

THE GIRL'S HOLLOW EYES HELD A DETACHED CURIOSITY AND maybe even cynicism. A *Mona Lisa* observance of him. "What are you doing? Why haven't you run away yet?"

"I can't leave you here." Andy flashed back to his leg hanging out of the window in the loft. To the gaping exit at the end of the corridor. He'd been so close to freedom. "I had to come back. You deserve a life. My little girl lost hers, and now

I have an opportunity to help you get the one you should be living. It doesn't bring her back, but it's something, right?"

Andy pulled Nell's keys from his pocket and found the most likely candidate. One twist and it unlocked with a gentle *click*. He left the girl to open the door herself and rushed to the small window. Unlike the one in his cell, this one had a latch. The action gritty with rust, it still turned easily enough. But when he shoved the window, it opened no more than an inch before halting. Another push yielded the same response. The grass outside had grown too long and thick. "Fuck it."

It didn't matter what Einstein said about insanity, Andy shoved the window again. And then again, each time with more force than before.

A clenched jaw, his stinging thigh fighting for more of his attention, Andy shook his head. "Fuck it."

Maybe the distance between Andy and the cannibals now prevented him from hearing them, or maybe they'd started their search. Would they check the basement again? He shoved the window harder than ever. The bloated frame splintered, his right hand slipping through the dirty pane with a *pop*. The glass tore a gash through his palm, blood turning his hand slick.

Footsteps beat against the floorboards in the main hallway. Andy shook, picking the damp and slippery shards of glass from the wooden frame. Most of it came away easily, but one particularly stubborn piece remained wedged in the wood. A jagged tooth coated in his blood. It would tear the girl to shreds. Several attempts to grip and pull it out, but his pinch slipped off every time.

The footsteps continued through the building. Shouldn't they all have gone outside by now? Drawing his bleeding hand into his sleeve, Andy used his makeshift glove to pinch the glass. It gave him enough purchase to wiggle the sharp shard free.

His hand still covered with his sleeve, Andy ran it around the remains of the frame. Nothing left to snag her, he reached out into the night and patted the grass as flat as he could. He turned to the girl, hunched down and made a step by interlocking his fingers. Blood ran from the back of his hand to the floor.

The girl hesitated. "But you won't fit."

"No," Andy said. He faced the stone stairs leading back to the ward.

"Then what will you do?"

"I have a plan. And that plan involves getting you out first, so hurry up." Before she said anything else, Andy added, "I want you to wait just outside. Find somewhere good to hide and wait until the adults are distracted. When that happens, run. Run with everything you have. Get to the closest house and ask them to call the police. You won't be in trouble, I promise. Just make sure you tell them *everything*, okay?"

The girl nodded.

"Don't hold anything back. *None* of this is your fault."

She nodded again. "How will I know when to run?"

"You'll hear it." After a pause, Andy said, "Can I give you a new name?"

"I'd love to have it. If you don't mind?"

Andy smiled at her. "Come on now." He flicked his head up to encourage her to climb.

Gwen stood on his hand, twisting her foot against the gash.

Andy groaned through the pain and boosted her out of the window.

ANDY DID HAVE A PLAN, WHICH WAS WHY HE TOLD HER AS much. Okay, so he hadn't revealed the extent of that plan, which had been realised when Gwen's pasty and emaciated form slipped into the dark night. Now he needed to think of something that would get him out of there too.

Back at the top of the stairs, Andy leaned against the wall, catching his breath from the short climb. The throb in his thigh had turned into a constant angry buzz that ran all the way to his bone marrow.

The thud of steps still searched the building despite their plans to head outside. Although there were clearly only a small percentage of the gang left in the place.

Now in the ward, Andy pulled back one of the sheets covering a window, wincing against the moonlight. The girl had vanished. Not an easy task for someone so pale and dressed in white.

And that was when the final part of the plan came to him. Smiling through his tears, Andy filled his lungs with the stagnant air. His voice echoed through the old building. If the girl remained close by, she'd probably hear him too. "You sick bastards! You're fucking wrong in the head, you know that?"

"He's inside," one of the voices in the woods shouted. "Come on."

As the footsteps descended on him, Andy smiled to watch a flash of white make her break and vanish into the dark depths of the surrounding woodland. "Good girl."

The approaching people growing louder, Andy held his right palm up and kissed the fingers before waving. "Bye, Gwen." He turned his back on the window and laughed despite the screaming burn of sitting down. He rested against the cold wall.

A man ran into the ward first. A few inches taller than Andy and much wider, he had a baseball bat in his grip, wild eyes, and sallow cheeks. Andy smiled. "Come on then, you fat fuck."

The large man's face twisted. He opened his mouth—the

streak of moonlight Andy had let in showing he had several teeth missing—and charged as more people entered the room behind him.

Andy maintained eye contact with the man who held his bat in a tight two-handed grip as he wound it back to swing.

EPILOGUE

Liz flinched when Andy stood up and charged. She knew what was coming and shivered from the cold rush of him passing straight through her. She'd never get used to that. Still cold, she turned around as he fell to his knees in front of the girl in the doorway. A lump rose in her throat when Andy reached up and held the little girl's hands.

"Gwen?" Andy said.

The girl couldn't have been any older than ten. Bald, skinny, and with black bags beneath her eyes. Her tiny legs were so thin she probably wouldn't have been able to stand at the end. "Daddy? Where am I?"

Liz drew a deep gulp and stepped forward. "I can help you." Her voice trembled when they both looked at her. "I can help you move on. Together."

Andy stood up and continued to hold one of his daughter's hands.

"I've been sent here today," Liz said, "because we have a little girl in custody who's telling us about a group of cannibals. I just need you to confirm the truth of it so we can put our case together against these vile creatures."

Andy's entire frame swelled. Were his eyes able to water, they would have filled at that moment. His voice weak, he said, "She made it?"

"Yes, and she's safe."

"Thank god. She was kept in a cage and they called her Worm. The only food they gave her was the flesh of people they caught. She had no choice." He nodded at his daughter. "I changed the girl's name to Gwen"—his face softened when he turned to his little girl—"the name of the most beautiful, smart, and funny girl I've ever known."

Liz smiled. "Thank you. That's all we needed. Now don't be afraid." Creating a white light in one of the room's doorways, she said, "When you walk through that, all of the pain and baggage you carry with you from your physical life will go away. You won't hurt anymore."

At that moment, Gwen's spirit fell over, buckling as she crashed to her knees.

Andy scooped her up in his arms and placed a gentle kiss on her forehead. She stared up at him. "I'm scared, Daddy."

While shaking his head, Andy said, "Don't be. We need to go to the light. We can leave the suffering behind."

Liz cried freely as the small child curled up in her dad's arms and rested her bald head against his chest. As the pair vanished through the doorway, she turned away from Bart, her tears falling from her chin. Sure, she got what the police needed from Andy, and she'd get paid, but times like this reminded her why she'd chosen her profession.

ENDS.

Support the Author

Dear reader, as an independent author I don't have the resources of a huge publisher. If you like my work and would like to see more from me in the future, there are two things you can do to help: leaving a review, and a word-of-mouth referral.

Releasing a book takes many hours and hundreds of dollars. I love to write, and would love to continue to do so. All I ask is that you leave a review. It shows other readers that you've enjoyed the book and will encourage them to give it a try too. The review can be just one sentence, or as long as you like.

You might also enjoy my other post-apocalyptic series - The Alpha Plague. Books 1-8 (the complete series) are available now.

The Alpha Plague - Available Now at
www.michaelrobertson.co.uk

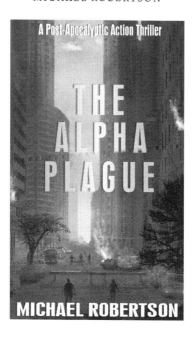

Or save money by picking up the entire series box set at
www.michaelrobertson.co.uk

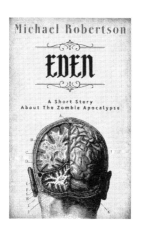

ABOUT THE AUTHOR

Like most children born in the seventies, Michael grew up with Star Wars in his life. An obsessive watcher of the films, and an avid reader from an early age, he found himself taken over with stories whenever he let his mind wander.

Those stories had to come out.

He hopes you enjoy reading his books as much as he does writing them.

Michael loves to travel when he can. He has a young family, who are his world, and when he's not reading, he enjoys walking so he can dream up more stories.

Contact
www.michaelrobertson.co.uk
subscribers@michaelrobertson.co.uk

Enigma - Book Six of The Shadow Order

Prophecy - Book Seven of The Shadow Order

The Faradis - Book Eight of The Shadow Order

The Complete Shadow Order Box Set

The Girl in the Woods - A Ghost's Story - Off-Killer Tales
Book One.

Masked - A Psychological Horror

Crash - A Dark Post-Apocalyptic Tale

Crash II: Highrise Hell

Crash III: There's No Place Like Home

Crash IV: Run Free

Crash V: The Final Showdown

New Reality: Truth

New Reality 2: Justice

New Reality 3: Fear

Printed in Poland
by Amazon Fulfillment
Poland Sp. z o.o., Wrocław